# the Sprog
# Time-Hopping Frog

Written by
Amanda Brandon

Illustrated by
Mariia Kolker

# Chapter 1

Sprog was the first frog who had ever jumped back in time. He set his time-hopper to leave the jungle he'd been visiting and return to his own time. **Beep! Beep! Beep!**

The dial on his belt flashed green.

Suddenly, the earth shook and he heard an enormous roar. He stumbled and fell backwards into the long grass. He peeped out. An enormous T-Rex was only a breath away.

It lifted its head to the sun. Sprog stared at its gleaming teeth. He kept as quiet as a mouse.

Any movement and he would be dinosaur lunch.

What could he do? His dial flashed green again.

He needed to jump within the next ten seconds.

It was now or never. Sprog bent his knees...

"One... two... three!" he quietly counted, then

leapt as high as he could...

# BOING!

The T-Rex was startled. The long-legged frog

pinged into the air.

"Agh!" Sprog cried as he peered

into the dinosaur's eyes.

# "RAAAAAAHHH!"

the dinosaur roared and tried to snap him up.
It missed, but it caught Sprog's controller and
sent him spinning in the air. Sprog pressed his
controller again.

**Whoosh!** Sprog zoomed out of reach.
He gave a huge sigh. But suddenly, he hurtled
towards earth, and everything turned black.

# Chapter 2

Sprog woke up and rubbed his head. He checked his legs and was relieved to find he was still in one piece. He heard voices and the clatter of horses' hooves. He smelled warm bread and honey. Honey?

This wasn't his riverbank home. He was in a marketplace. There were stalls selling pots and leather goods. Everyone wore tunics.

Some animals were carrying baskets or water urns.

Where was he? He looked down at his time-hopper belt. His eyes widened and he swallowed hard. The cover was smashed and the dial was jammed on Ancient Greece.

The T-Rex had damaged his controller. How was he going to get home now?

"Help! Stop it!" A small voice pleaded.

Sprog looked around. He spotted a tall, grinning weasel holding a clay pot. The owner of the pot, a small frog, was hopping up and down, trying to catch it. Then the weasel threw the pot and it smashed to the ground.

The weasel shook with laughter.

Sprog glared. He didn't like bullies. The weasel grabbed a large urn.

"Not that one," the small frog panted. He stretched up. "That's my best one."

The weasel spun the urn and lifted it high in the air.

Sprog sprang into action. He leapt just as the weasel released it. His webbed fingers caught the urn's handles before it hit the ground, and the weasel was knocked out of the way. The weasel rubbed his head and glared. "What the...?"

The little frog beamed. "Thank you, thank you!" he said.

The weasel slunk away, muttering. He glanced back at Sprog and scowled.

"I'm Linus," the little frog said, as Sprog helped sweep up the broken pot. "Otis always causes trouble. He thinks it's fun to tease. Thank you for jumping to help."

Sprog's green cheeks turned red. "It was nothing. I'm used to it. I have to leap to make my time-hopper work."

"Your time-hopper?" Linus's eyes goggled.

"Yes, I have a special time-hopper which allows me to go back and forth in time. In fact, I've just escaped from a dinosaur."

"Wow! That sounds super exciting! It's not much to repay you, but take one of my urns—I make them myself." Linus held out a small clay pot with black and red patterns.

Sprog shook his head. "Thank you, but I don't need any payment. What I need is to fix my controller. The dinosaur broke it. That's how I landed here."

He showed Linus the damaged controller on his belt. Linus looked in awe but shook his head. "I can fix broken pots but I don't know how to fix that, I'm afraid."

Sprog's shoulders drooped.

"But I do know someone who might. I've heard of a great inventor called Archimedes Toad who is staying near here. He made a device to measure distance. If there's anyone who might be able to fix your time-hopper, it's him."

"Archimedes Toad! I've heard of him," Sprog said. "But if he's so important, will he speak to an ordinary frog like me?"

# Chapter 3

"There's only one way to find out," Linus said. "I've never met Archimedes Toad but I'll take you to him. It's the least I can do. But first I've got to pack my things away."

Sprog helped Linus, then they set off. The sun dazzled Sprog's eyes and the heat made him wipe his brow. They passed several homes made out of wood and mud bricks before they reached the countryside. Finally, they came to a large house set in a courtyard. It had wooden shutters to keep the sun out. They knocked on the door, but there was no answer. Sprog knocked louder.

Finally, a shutter opened. Someone called, "Who's there?"

Sprog cleared his throat. "Err... Please, sir, I need your help. My device is broken."

"Sorry, I don't do repairs. You need the blacksmith in town. Good day."

A hand reached to pull the shutter.

"Wait," Sprog pleaded, "it's my time-hopping device. I know you are an important inventor.

Only you can help."

Sprog willed the door to open.

Linus held his breath.

There was a shuffling from inside. Finally, the door was opened by a large, green toad in a tunic and scruffy leather sandals. They were face to face with the famous inventor, Archimedes Toad. He peered down at them. "A time-hopper? How curious... In that case, you'd better come in."

Sprog and Linus followed him into a room packed with maps, tripods and tools.

Sprog unclipped his belt and showed Archimedes the damaged dial. He told him what

he'd told Linus. "...And the dinosaur damaged the setting. I have no way to get home." His voice trailed off and he gave a sob.

Linus squeezed his hand and whispered, "Don't worry, Archimedes is super clever. He'll fix it."

"Hmm... I wonder?" Archimedes said.

Sprog and Linus watched the inventor lift the broken cover, poke at the dial and rattle the time-hopper. He shook his head and frowned.

A screw fell out and bounced across the floor. Sprog cried out in alarm. He watched with anxious eyes as Archimedes hurried over to his maps and started to search. He seemed to forget

Sprog and Linus were there.

Finally, he returned.

"Yes, I think I can fix your time-hopper."

Sprog's hopes rose, until Archimedes added, "However, it won't be as good as new and you need to jump higher and further too in order to make it work. The question is: have you got the strength?"

# Chapter 4

Sprog and Linus left Archimedes working on the time-hopper and went to Linus's home for the night.

"This has been an exciting day, but I feel very tired," Linus yawned. Sprog agreed. After running from a dinosaur and their long walk to the inventor's house, he wasn't sure he had much strength left at all!

"Don't worry," Linus said, "I'll help you get stronger. I'm entering our town's Champion Games. We hold them in honour of the gods. I have to practise running, discus, long jump and boxing. We can train together."

They made a start the next day at the gym. They warmed up by jogging on the spot, followed by some short sprints.

"I fancy a run first," Sprog said.

"We have to do it in armour," Linus added.

"It's the rules." He handed Sprog a helmet and a

breastplate. They were very heavy.

Sprog couldn't keep going for long. "This is

too hard..."

He puffed and collapsed on the ground next to Linus, who had tripped over when his helmet fell over his eyes.

The long, lean body of Otis the weasel dashed past. "Losers." He grinned.

Next, they tried boxing. A jab here... a jab there... Sprog was on the ground.

"Oops, sorry," Linus said when he punched too hard.

When he stopped feeling dizzy, Sprog said, "Let's try the discus. That can't be too hard."

But the discs were heavy. They sailed through the air and landed with a splash in the fountain.

Otis watched and laughed. "That was useless.

Face it: you won't beat me!"

Sprog scowled.  He didn't like being laughed at.

He knew he could do better. He vowed to prove

Otis wrong.

# Chapter 5

A few days later, Sprog and Linus returned to Archimedes Toad.

"I can't wait to see your time-hopper in action," Linus bounced up and down and grinned. Then his face fell. "Although I expect it means you'll be whizzing off home soon."

"Let's see what happens," Sprog said briskly.

He thought of the green grass and cool water of his riverbank home. Ancient Greece was very hot. Too hot for him. But he didn't want to admit he was homesick when Linus had been so kind.

Archimedes greeted them with a cheerful wave and welcomed them into his workroom.

Sprog spotted his time-hopper belt on the desk. It looked like his old time-hopper but the dial had changed and the cover was now made of leather.

"To make your controller work you have to hold down the lever for longer and jump harder," Archimedes said. "The workings have been

strained and I don't have all the materials to replace them."

Sprog nodded. At last, he would be going home. But Archimedes said, "Before you use it, I must test the spring in your jump. As I said, you have to leap extra high."

"Okay," Sprog said. They went outside. Archimedes counted, "One... two... three!"

Sprog bent his knees and leapt. His feet left marks in the dusty ground as he landed.

"Try again," Archimedes said. Sprog crouched even lower and tried again.

Archimedes scratched his head and sighed.

"I'm sorry, that's not good enough. You won't be able to make the time-hopper work until you leap higher and further."

Sprog blinked back tears. He couldn't jump high enough. Perhaps he would be stuck in Ancient Greece forever.

# Chapter 6

"Don't worry, we'll think of something," Linus said, as they went to bed that night. He was soon fast asleep, but Sprog tossed and turned. He wondered how he could improve his leaping.

The next morning, they rose early. Linus wanted to put in some more training, so they went to the gymnasium. There were lots of others working out for the Champion Games.

Sprog looked over at some rats jumping in the sand. Their bodies were long but their feet were small. They took tiny jumps.

Linus noticed them too and said, "You would be great at the long jump with your stretchy legs."

Sprog clapped his head. "That's it! I should practise long jump to help me jump further and higher. It will make my legs strong enough to use my time-hopper."

So together they practised and practised and practised. Days passed and Sprog felt his long legs grow stronger and stronger. He really hoped this would be enough to finally hop home!

A few days later, Sprog and Linus visited Archimedes Toad to show him what Sprog could do.

On the dusty ground outside, Sprog hopped his longest jump yet! He held his breath nervously while he waited for Archimedes's decision.

The toad scribbled his notes down before he broke into a wide grin. "You did it, Sprog! You're finally ready."

Sprog beamed. Linus smiled too, but Sprog noticed that his smile didn't reach his eyes and he was poking the ground with his toe.

Sprog said, "I'll hop off soon, but first I must see Linus compete in the Champion Games."

The little frog's face lit up and he said to Sprog, "Thank you! You should have a go too."

Soon, it was time for the Games! The gym was full of cheering animals in the audience and other competitors warming up. Sprog and Linus stretched before signing up for their own sports. Linus put his name down for boxing, and Sprog signed up for the long jump, of course!

Archimedes came and cheered them both. Sprog made sure to let Archimedes look after his time-hopper... He didn't want to break it again! Linus and Sprog wished each other luck and waved to Archimedes.

Linus managed to beat Otis in the boxing,
although he didn't reach the final, and Sprog
was awarded a winner's olive leaf wreath for his
amazing long jump.

He gave it to Linus. "This is to say thank you for helping. I couldn't have done it without you."

Linus gave Sprog one of his homemade urns—it had a picture of the two of them jumping.

"This will remind you of Greece. You could have hopped off when your controller was fixed but you stayed to take part in the Games with me. I didn't win but I gained something far better: a good friend."

The two hugged. Sprog promised, "I'll hop back and see you again one day... or maybe Archimedes will create another time-hopper so you can join me on my adventures!"

Linus jumped in the air and said, "Now that definitely sounds super!"

Sprog pressed his time-hopper and leapt into the sky. At last, he was on his way home!

# Discussion Points

**1.** Where is Sprog in the beginning?

**2.** Who smashes Linus's urns?

**a)** Sprog

**b)** Archimedes

**c)** Otis

**3.** What was your favourite part of the story?

**4.** What does Sprog practise to help him jump further?

**5.** Why do you think Sprog and Linus struggled to run in armour?

**6.** Who was your favourite character and why?

**7.** There were moments in the story when Sprog had to **get stronger**. Where do you think the story shows this most?

**8.** What do you think happens after the end of the story?

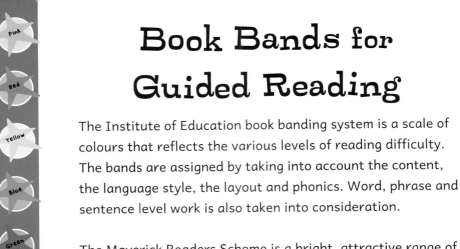

# Book Bands for Guided Reading

The Institute of Education book banding system is a scale of colours that reflects the various levels of reading difficulty. The bands are assigned by taking into account the content, the language style, the layout and phonics. Word, phrase and sentence level work is also taken into consideration.

The Maverick Readers Scheme is a bright, attractive range of books covering the pink to grey bands. All of these books have been book banded for guided reading to the industry standard and edited by a leading educational consultant.

To view the whole Maverick Readers scheme, visit our website at

www.maverickearlyreaders.com

Or scan the QR code to view our scheme instantly!

# Maverick Chapter Readers
## (From Lime to Grey Band)